This Walker book belongs to:

_____

_____

_____

_____

For Sally

P. P. & H. C.

First published 2013 by Walker Books Ltd, 87 Vauxhall Walk, London SE11 5HJ • This edition published 2014 • 10 9 8 7 6 5 4 3 2 1
Text © 2013 Philippa Pearce • Illustrations © 2013 Helen Craig • The right of Philippa Pearce and Helen Craig to be identified as author and illustrator
respectively of this work has been asserted by them in accordance with the Copyright, Designs and Patents Act 1988 • This book has been typeset in Stempel Schneidler
• Printed in China • All rights reserved. No part of this book may be reproduced, transmitted or stored in an information retrieval system in any form or by any
means, graphic, electronic or mechanical, including photocopying, taping and recording, without prior written permission from the publisher. • British Library
Cataloguing in Publication Data: a catalogue record for this book is available from the British Library • ISBN 978-1-4063-5261-0 • www.walker.co.uk

Amy's Three Best Things

Philippa Pearce

Illustrated by
Helen Craig

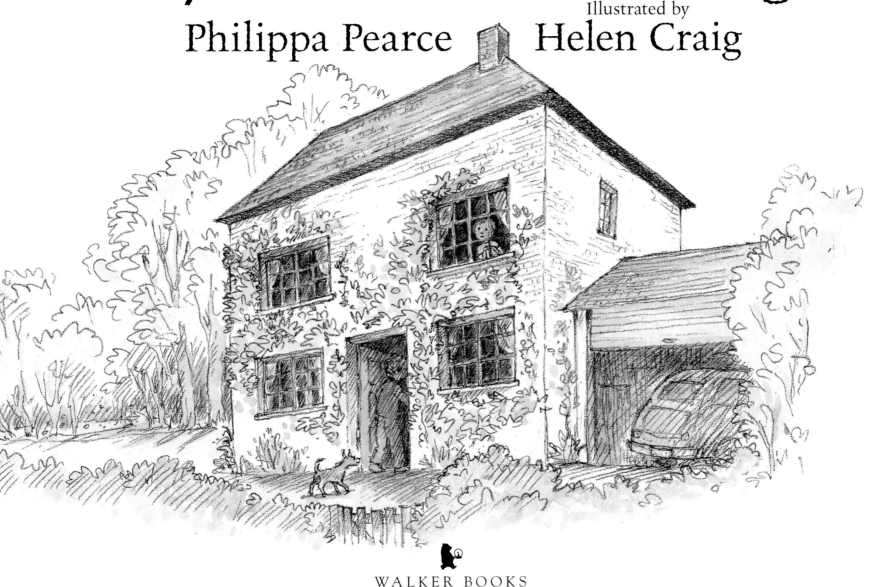

WALKER BOOKS
AND SUBSIDIARIES
LONDON • BOSTON • SYDNEY • AUCKLAND

One day Amy said,

"I'd like to go and see Granny soon. I'd like to go all by myself, and I'd like to stay the night."

Her mother said, "Are you sure, Amy?" For Amy had not been away from home by herself before.

"Of course, I'm sure," Amy said crossly. "In fact, I'll stay two nights. No, I'll stay three."

Amy packed her bag with her teddy and
her pyjamas and all the other ordinary things
she needed. Then she put in three more
things. One thing came from the floor
beside her bed; another thing came
from the mantelpiece in her bedroom;

and the third thing came
from the rack over the bath
in the bathroom.

Those are my three best
things for a visit, she thought.

"What will you do while I'm away?" Amy asked her mother.

"Well, this evening I have to cut the grass," her mother said.

"What will Bill and Bonzo be doing?"

"Bill will be in bed. Asleep, I hope. Bonzo will be somewhere chewing a stick."

"I just wanted to know," said Amy.

At Granny's house, Amy unpacked her bag. But she didn't take out her three best things, because they were secret. She and Granny spent the rest of the afternoon spring-cleaning Granny's old toy-cupboard. Amy found it extremely interesting. Then it was time for tea and bed.

Amy soon fell asleep, but later she woke. It was still daylight. She missed her mother and Bill and Bonzo. She wanted her own home.

Then she remembered her three best things. She got out of bed and fetched the first one: a little stripy mat from the floor beside her bed at home.

Amy laid the mat on the floor by her bed in Granny's house. She sat on the edge of the bed with her feet on the mat.

At first Amy didn't feel any better. Then she noticed a tingling in her feet. She stood up on the mat. It seemed to shift beneath her. She sat down on the mat only just in time, for it was beginning to move.

The mat was rising, slowly at first. Then, in a rush, it rose much higher. It flew towards the window, and the window opened and Amy on her magic mat sailed out into the summer air.

The mat flew smoothly and fast in the direction of home. And there was her house, and there was the garden, and her mother had just finished mowing the lawn. She was scolding Bonzo, who had chewed up a stick all over the new-cut grass.

Then Amy wanted to see what Bill was doing, and the mat took her to his bedroom window. There was Bill asleep in his cot with his knitted rabbit held up to his cheek.

Amy wasn't feeling unhappy any more. The mat turned and carried her back as swiftly as before – back to her granny's house, in through the window and down to the floor by Amy's bed.

It was just an ordinary little stripy mat again.

The next day Amy and her granny
had a picnic lunch in the park,
and Granny bought ice-creams
to finish off the lunch. The sun
shone, and Amy went into the
playground and swung and
climbed and slid and twirled.
They came back late and tired.

That night, Amy fell asleep
quickly; but moonlight on her
face woke her. She sat up, missing
home all over again. She missed
her mother and Bill and Bonzo.

Then she remembered her three best things. She got out of bed and fetched the second one: a tiny wooden horse from her mantelpiece at home.

Amy put the tiny horse on the floor, and at once it began to grow. As it grew, it pawed the ground and snorted with impatience.

When the horse was the right size, Amy climbed on to its back, and the horse set off at a gallop through the air – out of the window and into the moonshiny night. It whinnied for joy as it rushed towards Amy's house.

As late as this, everyone would be indoors. Amy looked into the sitting-room. There sat her mother, watching television, with Bonzo snoozing at her feet. In his bedroom, Bill was also asleep, with his knitted rabbit at his cheek.

And now the horse tossed its mane and set off back to Granny's house. It galloped all the way and in through Amy's window and down to her bedside.

Then it was just a tiny wooden horse again. Amy picked it up and put it safely on the mantelpiece.

The next day Amy and her granny stayed mostly indoors, because it rained. They made a cake together. It was a splendid cake, and a large one. They iced it, and Amy decorated it with sugar-flowers and jelly babies and hundreds-and-thousands.

"Perfect for tomorrow," said Granny, "when your mother comes with Bill and Bonzo, to take you home. There'll be a fair in town, too, and we could all go together, before you leave."

"I'd like that," said Amy. "I'd like that very much. And then, after the fair, I'll say goodbye to you and I'll get in the car with the others and I'll go home."

"That's it," said Granny.

That night Amy fell asleep to the sound of
rain. Later, thunder and lightning woke her. She
sat up, thinking what a long way off tomorrow
seemed. She wanted her mother and Bill and
Bonzo *now*.

Then she remembered her three best things.
She got out of bed and fetched the third: a little
wooden boat from the bathroom at home.

As she looked, the boat began to grow, then
to rock as though it were riding on water. When
it was big enough, Amy stepped in. The boat
rose and sailed out through the window, into the
stormy night. Amy was not afraid of the storm,
and the rain did not even damp her pyjamas.

Through the whistling winds and rushing rain, the boat took Amy to her home. She looked in through the sitting-room window, but the television was switched off. There was no one there, not even Bonzo. No one was in Bill's room either – his cot was empty.

At last Amy looked in the garage and – sure enough, as she had feared – the car was gone. Then she knew that all her family had gone away without her. She flung herself down in the bottom of the boat, and cried.

The boat slewed round and started off the way it had come. It took Amy back to her granny's house, in through the window, and then was just a little bathroom boat again on the floor. Amy stood beside it and cried and cried.

From downstairs Amy heard the sound of people talking:
Granny had visitors. But Amy did not care if they heard her.
From downstairs, someone – it wasn't her granny – said,
"Hush!" Then, quite clearly, Amy heard her mother's voice: "It's
Amy crying!" Then there were footsteps hurrying upstairs and
the bedroom door was flung open and her mother was kneeling
beside her, asking, "Amy, whatever is the matter?"

"I missed you all," said Amy, still crying because she
couldn't stop at once.

"Well, here we all are," said her mother. "We
came tonight instead of tomorrow." She
tucked Amy up, and kissed her goodnight.
"Tomorrow, if it's fine, we'll go to the fair."

And the next day the sun shone, so they all went to the fair.

Amy's favourite thing at the fair was the old-fashioned merry-go-round. When the music played, all the animals moved up and down, and round in their big circle.

Amy chose to ride a dragon. When the music started, she clung on tight and waved goodbye to her family. Then the merry-go-round swirled her off so that she could no longer see them. But she knew they would still be there when she came round again.

Bill was laughing and waving both hands; and Amy waved back.

Round and round went the merry-go-round with Amy on her dragon; and sometimes she saw her family and sometimes she didn't.

But they were always there.

More books from Philippa Pearce and Helen Craig:

ISBN 978-0-7445-9481-2

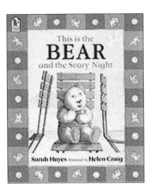

ISBN 978-0-7445-9482-9

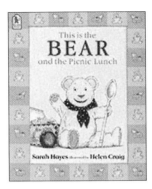

ISBN 978-0-7445-9811-7

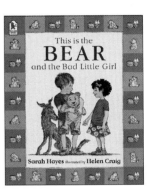

ISBN 978-0-7445-9812-4

ISBN 978-1-4063-1982-8

ISBN 978-1-4063-2349-8

Available from all good booksellers

www.walker.co.uk